The Seoul subway network is one of the longest in the world and reaches far beyond the city limits. If you were to include all the lines that extend outside the city, it would easily be the longest subway in the world. It carries an average of 7.2 million people per day on the city lines alone. Korean names are usually three syllables, starting with the surname and followed by two personal names. You'll see lots of these as you meet the people in this book.

I rattle and clatter over the tracks.

Same time, same route, every day.

Carrying people from one place to another,

I travel over the ground and rumble under,
twice across the wide Han River.

Around I go, around and around.
Crowds of people wait to climb aboard.

ba-dum, ba-dum

I AM THE SUBWAY

words & illustrations by Kim Hyo-eun
translated by Deborah Smith

SCRIBBLE

I pull into a station
ba-dum, ba-dum
and those who were sleeping startle awake.
ba-dum, ba-dum
Is this your stop? It's time to get off!

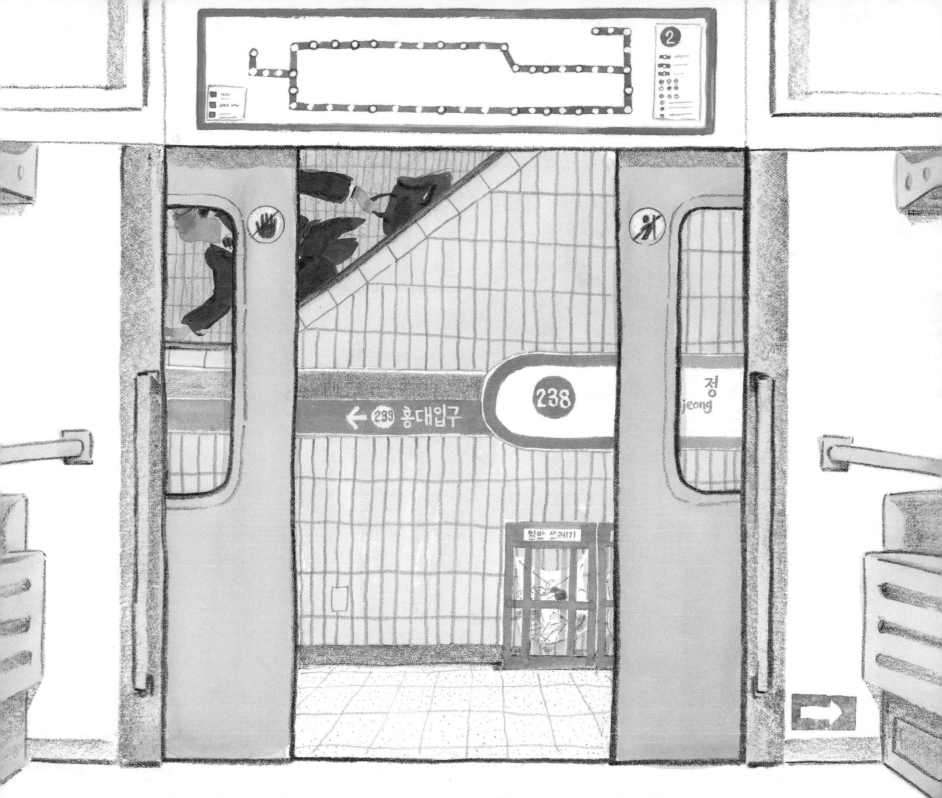

This station is Hapjeong, Hapjeong station.
There's Mr. Wanju, running for the train. Quick, Mr. Wanju!

I'm running late again; I don't want to miss my train.
Dashing past other people, through the ticket stile,
I take the stairs three or four at a time,
all the way to the platform!

In school I could win the relay race
even when my team was coming last.
These days, my lovely daughter makes me late for work.
At the end of the day I always leave first,
to run home and see her smile.

Mr. Wanju sits down and checks his watch,
gets his breath back and smiles, knowing everything's fine.
Time for me to set off again, with these busy hearts on board.

ba-dum, ba-dum, ba-dum, ba-dum
This station is City Hall, City Hall station.
Again, my doors open — who is it now?
Granny brings the strong, salty smell of the sea.

Me, I was born and grew up by the ocean.
The sea was stern, like my father,
and generous, like my mother.
The sea taught me a lot:
I've learned to stay afloat in happiness
and in sadness.

I love to bring fresh fish to my family in Seoul.
Octopus is my daughter's favorite dish
and my granddaughter likes abalone.
I'm going to cook a feast for my girls!

Granny clutches her bundle tightly
while I bob gently along, carrying their joy —
Granny, her daughter, and her daughter's daughter.

ba-dum, ba-dum, ba-dum, ba-dum
This station is Seongsu, Seongsu station.
I'm happy to see two new passengers — but wait, it's three!

"Is that Yu-seon?"
"Hi, Mom ..."

I'm my mom's baby girl,
Yu-seon, Jung Yu-seon.

Yu-seon the cry-baby, sleepy-head, scaredy-cat
now has two babies of her own!
I hold this family all in my embrace.

ba-dum, ba-dum, ba-dum, ba-dum
This station is Guui, Guui station.
Someone strides in proudly with well-shined shoes.
It's Mr. Jae-sung from Guro—I remember him.

Sneakers that like to splash through muddy puddles,
black shoes that hurry to the office every morning,
new shoes saved for a special day,
battered cast-offs re-heeled and patched—
I can tell so much about a person just
from looking at their shoes.
   All kinds find their way to my door—
      shoes that have traveled near and far.

Mr. Jae-sung's gaze shifts from his newspaper to other people's shoes.
He thinks he can guess the paths they might have walked.

ba-dum, ba-dum, ba-dum, ba-dum
This station is Gangnam, Gangnam station.
And here's Na-yoon — I wonder how she's been?
Whoa there, remember to look where you're going!

In the mid-term exams I was 5th in my class
and 48th in the school;
in the finals I came 12th and 103rd.
My grades go up and down like a roller-coaster.
Every day I have all these after-school classes:
one hour of math, two hours of English,
and an hour and a half of essay writing.
I haul myself up and down these tall buildings
while my mood goes up and down too.

I'm happy to see her,
but Na-yoon's so tired she's barely awake.
As I set off, poor Na-yoon's feelings are as heavy as her bag.

ba-dum, ba-dum, ba-dum, ba-dum
Mr. Gu looks embarrassed. I can see him blush
as he pushes his cart into the carriage.

"Ladies and gentlemen, may I please have your attention!
I have an amazing new product I know you're going to love!

These gloves will keep your hands toasty warm, no nasty grazes if you fall over,
they can be worn by adults or children, one size fits all.
All the colors of the rainbow, there's no color I don't have. Just 1,000 won each!"

I run along the rails with a rainbow-colored mind.

ba-dum, ba-dum, ba-dum, ba-dum
This station is Sillim, Sillim station.
Now, who do we have this time?

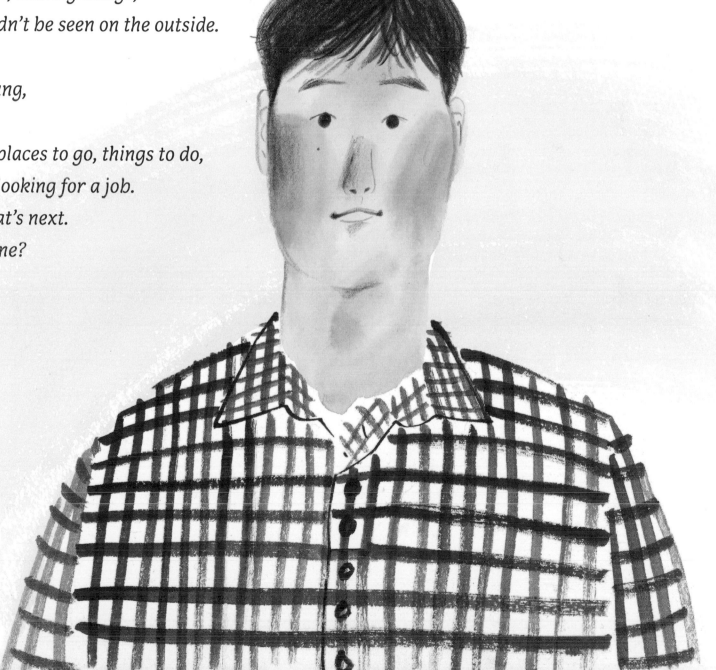

When I was born,
my father gave me a beautiful name:
Do meaning 'ceramic', young meaning 'jade marble'.
He chose this name so my heart would be
filled with bright, shining things,
even if this couldn't be seen on the outside.

I am Lee Do-young,
29 this year.
Everybody has places to go, things to do,
but not me. I'm looking for a job.
I'm not sure what's next.
Who will I become?

Do-young offers his arm to Yeon-woo, the little boy sliding around.
Yeon-woo hides his face and Do-young gives him a gentle smile.

ba-dum, ba-dum
ba-du-bum, ba-dum

I run in one big ring around the city of Seoul each day,
sending people off and welcoming them on.

ba-dum, ba-dum
ba-dum, ba-dum

This station is Sindorim, Sindorim station.
The doors will open on your left.

On my travels I meet
so many people and things:

an old lady telling stories
in the market amid the
noise of buying and selling;

the scent of fried chicken,
crispy and hot,
shared by a dad and
his son as a special treat;

passengers sending messages
to friends and family;
the sour smell of sweat on
the long way home;

a gentle afternoon light that washes over everything —
old shoes, new shoes, clean and dull shoes.

The unique lives of strangers
you might never meet again

ba-dum, ba-dum, ba-dum, ba-dum

are all around you, every time you take the train.

About the author

I am Kim Hyo-eun. Hyo as in dawn, eun as in divine grace.
It is the name my father, at 32, gave to his second daughter.
I was born, and three younger siblings followed after. In
this way, I became daughter, younger sister, onni (older
sister to a girl), and nuna (older sister to a boy).

The seven of us went many places in my father's old car. We
saw pretty pebbles and small fish in valley streams so cold
they made your teeth chatter. We lay in ugly tents on the
beach and heard the sound of waves rolling in, overlapping.
Dark nights when the grasshoppers cried, on roads without
a single light, we encountered numberless stars, and the
white moon shining on each other's faces. We grew up
seeing the many things our father showed us.

At some point I became an adult, found the path I would
walk, and went down it. I saw the things I wanted to see,
passed by what was otherwise, pretending I couldn't see
it, and walked on diligently. Then all of a sudden I saw the
people on the path. I began to put wrinkled hands, different
colored faces, arms making various gestures, into pictures.
As the pictures accumulated steadily, I too wanted to show
them to someone, just as my father had showed us children
when we were young. Things I had seen on the path, things
that were near at hand but could not be seen, things not
visible to the eye but still significant.

About the translator

I am Deborah Smith. I grew up in a small South Yorkshire
town without a bookshop or books at home, never traveling.
I read translations, learned Korean, then began to translate
and founded Tilted Axis Press (publishing translations of
writing from across Asia), all to learn, share, and support
a more nuanced and equitable awareness of our mutually
entangled lives.

These days I translate little and slowly, mainly poetry.
My other translation work involves mentoring, curating,
and learning to live in India.

The illustrations in this book were made using watercolor paint.

Typeset in Excelsior and Capucine by the publisher.

Scribble, an imprint of Scribe Publications
18–20 Edward Street, Brunswick, Victoria 3056, Australia
2 John Street, Clerkenwell, London, WC1N 2ES, United Kingdom
3754 Pleasant Ave, Suite 100, Minneapolis, Minnesota 55409 USA

Originally published in Korean as 나는 지하철입니다 (*Naneun jihacheolimnida*)
by Munhakdongne Publishing Group, 2016

This edition published by Scribble, 2021

This book is printed with vegetable-soy based inks, on FSC® certified paper
and other controlled material from responsibly managed forests,
ensuring that the supply chain from forest to end-user is chain of custody certified.

MIX
Paper from
responsible sources
FSC® C016973

Printed and bound in China by 1010
9781922310514 (Australian hardback)
9781913348588 (UK hardback)
9781950354658 (US hardback)

Catalogue records for this title are available from the
National Library of Australia and the British Library

scribblekidsbooks.com
scribblekidsbooks

We acknowledge the Wurundjeri People of the Kulin Nation are the first and continuing custodians
of the land on which our books are created. Sovereignty has never been ceded.
We pay our respects to Elders past, present, and emerging, and to all First Nations people.